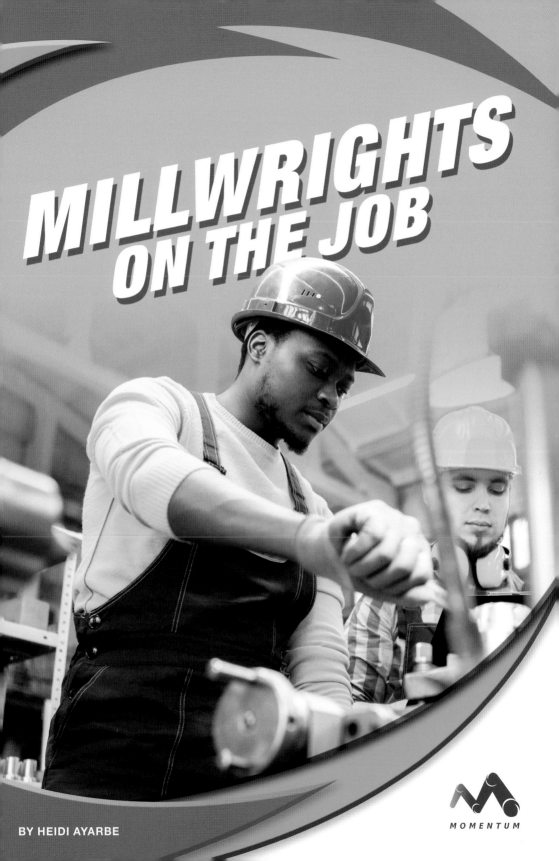

MILLWRIGHTS
ON THE JOB

BY HEIDI AYARBE

MOMENTUM

The Child's World®
childsworld.com

Published by The Child's World®
1980 Lookout Drive • Mankato, MN 56003-1705
800-599-READ • www.childsworld.com

Content Consultant: Shane Stockham, Industrial
Mechanics/Millwright Instructor, North Idaho
College

Photographs ©: SeventyFour/Shutterstock
Images, cover, 1; Michael Jung/Shutterstock
Images, 5; iStockphoto, 6, 9, 21, 28; Chayapol
Plairaharn/Shutterstock Images, 8; Highwaystarz
Photography/iStockphoto, 11; Monkey Business
Images/iStockphoto, 12; Science Photo/
Shutterstock Images, 14; Sol Stock/iStockphoto,
15; Shutterstock Images, 16, 18; Peter Gudella/
Shutterstock Images, 20; Bart Co/iStockphoto, 23;
Joni Hanebutt/Shutterstock Images, 24; Everett
Historical/Shutterstock Images, 26; Dobo Kristian/
Shutterstock Images, 27

ISBN 9781503835498
LCCN 2019943071

Printed in the United States of America

CONTENTS

MOMENTUM

FAST FACTS

What's the Job?

► Millwrights install, take apart, fix, put together, and move machines in places such as factories, power plants, and construction sites.

► Most millwrights work in manufacturing facilities or in construction.

► Millwrights need a high school diploma. They also can go to school for two years and get an associate's degree. In addition, many millwrights learn their trade through **apprenticeship** programs.

Important Stats

► In 2018, there were approximately 43,810 millwrights in the United States.

► The average yearly salary for millwrights in 2018 was $56,250.

► By 2026, jobs for millwrights, industrial machinery mechanics, and machinery maintenance workers are expected to grow by 7 percent.

It can take days and sometimes even ► weeks to put together a machine.

CHAPTER ONE

FROM GRANDFATHER CLOCKS TO FACTORIES

J avier had always been fascinated with grandfather clocks. His family had a tall one in the corner of their living room. As a child, he would watch the gold-colored **pendulum** swing back and forth in a steady rhythm. He would watch his mother raise the weights of the clock's **pulley** with a crank. Grandfather clocks need to be wound in order to work properly. Javier loved the machinery and how everything worked together.

One day, his mother moved the clock to another room. The clock stopped working correctly. The beat wasn't steady anymore. His mother was going to call a repairman, but Javier asked her to let him try to fix it. He watched the pendulum and saw that it brushed against the chime rods toward the back. The clock wasn't level. He leveled the clock, and it worked again.

◄ **Machines, such as clocks, have lots of gears inside to make them work.**

▲ **Blueprints are helpful when trying to figure out how things work.**

Javier liked to take things apart and put them back together. He set up a little shop in his family's garage. He became the neighborhood fixer. But he never thought the work he did could become a career. Years passed, and his high school graduation approached. Javier didn't know what to do after high school.

Everything changed during his high school's career day. Javier met a millwright. Javier had never even heard the word before. The millwright talked about his job. He had worked at factories, on construction sites, and with industrial machinery. He talked about solving problems and reading technical plans and **blueprints**. He showed Javier a technical plan. Javier visualized the layout of the machine. He tried to understand how each part worked to create a whole.

▲ **The UBC is a union. Unions aim to improve working conditions, payment, and hours for workers.**

After graduating, Javier filled out an application to become an apprentice with the United Brotherhood of Carpenters and Joiners of America (UBC). The UBC is one organization that educates and trains workers for various careers—including millwrights. Both women and men become millwrights. Javier also took a welding classes at the local community college. Millwrights use welding skills and many other trade skills to assemble machinery and equipment. Javier had a lot to learn.

The road to become a millwright is similar to many other trade jobs. Millwrights usually complete a three-to-four-year apprenticeship program. Each year, they complete more than 100 hours of technical instruction and at least 2,000 hours of paid, on-the-job training. They must learn many things such as welding, technical math, and machinery installation.

As an apprentice, Javier worked with and learned from a **journey worker** millwright for years. After each job, Javier became more confident about his skills. One morning, Javier and the journey worker were sent to a food processing plant. They had to figure out a problem. Something was slowing the machines down. That meant the plant wasn't filling the orders on time. It looked like they would have to take apart one of the conveyers. Conveyers are a series of belts that are connected. They transport items from station to station. If one conveyer slows down, everything slows down. Javier and the journey worker would have to take apart, label, and organize the machine. Production could come to a halt. The factory manager paced the cement floors. He was worried about the machines not working.

Javier and the journey worker checked the conveyer belt. Javier remembered his family's grandfather clock. He checked the pulleys. Javier noticed the head pulley had worn down.

▲ **Working with an experienced professional is a great way for an apprentice to learn.**

The belt was slipping. Javier talked to the journey worker and pointed out the problem. They would have to replace the belt.

Javier had one more year left in his apprenticeship. After completing his work hours and required classes, Javier could become a journey worker. He would be able to work independently or be hired at another organization. Javier knew what he learned during his time as an apprentice would help him for the rest of his career.

CHAPTER TWO

IN THE CLASSROOM

Quinn felt as though there was a knot tied in his stomach. He looked over his lesson plans twice. He drummed his fingers against his leg and checked his watch for a fourth time. Then, he walked toward the high school workshop. Late afternoon sunshine gleamed on the metal door handles. They were warm to the touch. Quinn had worked on construction sites and at food manufacturing plants as a millwright. He had also worked with oil companies and at automobile plants.

Quinn thought about his high school shop teacher, Mr. Pickrell. He remembered how Mr. Pickrell's salt-and-pepper-colored eyebrows would narrow together over the bridge of his nose if students weren't paying attention or working hard. Quinn always enjoyed shop class. He spent afternoons helping his teacher clean the shop. Mr. Pickrell taught him how to weld.

◄ **The right classes can successfully teach people who are interested in becoming millwrights.**

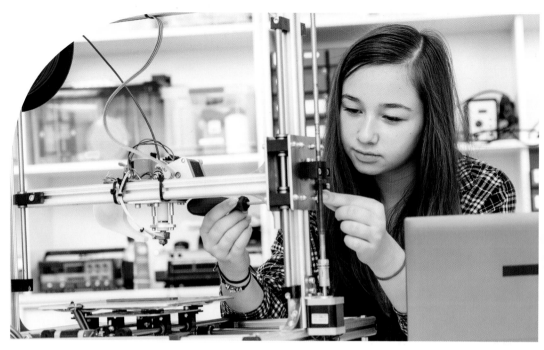

▲ **High schoolers can take classes, like electronics, to learn skills they need to become millwrights.**

He also taught Quinn how to clean the shop equipment. Mr. Pickrell encouraged Quinn to apply for a millwright apprenticeship. Mr. Pickrell pushed Quinn to be his best. Quinn always said he would go back to the classroom. Maybe he could help a kid, like Mr. Pickrell had helped him.

After years of working as a millwright, Quinn was ready to give back. When the opening for a shop teacher came up at his old high school, he had applied. Quinn even reached out to Mr. Pickrell for advice—this time on how to teach kids.

People who want to be millwrights ▶ should be good at math.

Quinn pushed the doors open and walked into the shop. He hoped no one would notice the beads of nervous sweat on his temples. Metal stools screeched across the cement floor as students took their seats. Staring at him were 20 sets of eyes. Quinn cleared his throat and asked his students if they were ready to learn.

Programs in high schools and trade schools often hire millwrights to teach. Their experience on the job is important in the classroom. They also teach students problem solving and basic blueprint reading. They teach students what they need to know to be successful as millwrights, or many other trades.

Machines are everywhere. Millwrights are needed in maintaining, repairing, assembling, and moving machines when needed. Qualified professionals are needed to train the next generation of millwrights in programs at high schools and technical schools. Millwrights can work almost anywhere. The technology will change, and the job might change, but the need for millwrights will not.

◄ **People can work together to fix issues with machines.**

CHAPTER THREE

MILLWRIGHTS AND TREATMENT PLANTS

C harlie and his crew drove through the gates of a wastewater treatment plant. Early that morning they had received an emergency call from the plant. The people there thought something might be wrong with the machines, because the plant wasn't working as well as it should. As Charlie drove into the plant, he saw rows of large, circular tanks of water. He knew that these tanks were part of the water cleaning process. They took sludge out of the water.

The treatment plant had many different types of machines, such as pumps and fans. Each one was needed to turn millions of gallons of wastewater into water that was safe to go back into rivers, lakes, and people's homes. Without these treatment plants, people could get very sick from dirty water.

◄ **A lot of different machines are used in wastewater treatment plants.**

▲ **Wastewater treatment plants take things such as food, chemicals, and human waste out of water.**

Before starting the repair work, Charlie talked to the operators. He asked questions about the equipment and maintenance. He and the crew checked the **maintenance logs**. They compared maintenance work with the operating manuals. Sometimes maintenance workers or operators don't follow the operating manual instructions. This can cause the machines to not work as well as they should. It can even cause machines to stop working.

This was the first time Charlie and his team had come to the plant. They looked at how the plant was originally organized.

▲ **It's important that millwrights wear proper safety gear, such as safety glasses, while on the job.**

They compared it to how the plant worked now. That would help them see if there was a problem because of changes that were made over time. This part of the work could be slow. But understanding how the plant was supposed to work was important to finding a solution to any problems.

Charlie realized there was a problem with the pumps. If a pump is clogged or has a leak, sewage could spill out of the tubes and **contaminate** the nearby rivers.

Charlie checked the valves, pump pressure, and sludge return. He discovered the pump filters were clogged with sludge. The pump filters needed to be changed. In the maintenance work log, somebody had calculated the wrong date for swapping out the filters. The filter upgrade was overdue. The millwright crew found the problem and helped get the treatment plant working efficiently once again.

Every day was different for Charlie and his team. For example, earlier that month, they had been hired by production plant managers to help design a new warehouse layout. Millwrights are often hired to make factories or plants work more efficiently. Charlie and his crew worked with a digital design program to get the job done. They showed their clients more logical ways to set up machines for maximum efficiency. With new floor plans, he and his crew recovered floor space to make room for new machines.

When machines are running correctly at a wastewater ▶ treatment plant, the water can be cleaned properly.

CHAPTER FOUR

THE FUTURE OF MILLWRIGHTS

Jessica pulled up to the dome-shaped building of the National Aeronautics and Space Administration (NASA) Glenn Research Center. The center was in Ohio, and Jessica was starting work before the sun had fully risen. The purple sky faded with the last glimmer of stars. The first light of day stretched across the sky, coloring the bellies of clouds orange.

Jessica turned off her car engine. She sipped her coffee and looked over at a Shuttle-Centaur booster. It was a piece of NASA's technology. The booster was developed by the research center and had been vital to space exploration in the 1960s and 1970s. Versions of it had been used for more than 50 years. Centaurs were boosters that launched satellites and rockets out of Earth's orbit. Now one of the boosters sat proudly next to Glenn Research Center.

◄ **NASA has been around since 1958.**

▲ **Micrometers help millwrights measure small distances.**

Jessica walked into the workroom with other millwrights. Jessica's tool box included micrometers, measuring tapes, lasers, and **precision**-measuring devices. The facility was almost always buzzing with energy. But that morning, it was quieter. The research center was in its annual maintenance shutdown. Once a year, the NASA facility closed its doors to check all its equipment.

◄ **Rocket boosters help spacecraft lift into space.**

▲ Having working machines is important for many
businesses in the United States today.

That meant the millwrights had extra work. The schedules were tight. They had to remove, reinstall, and relocate equipment. Jessica and her team made sure the machines were working well. The machines made it possible for scientists to study the galaxy, send scientists to the International Space Station, send a rover to Mars, and more.

New technology and machines are needed in all kinds of fields. With technological advances, qualified people are needed to maintain, repair, assemble, and transport machinery. Today, millwrights work in many different industries, including in aerospace and at construction and mining companies. Also, millwrights work with machines that provide **renewable energy**. Millwrights are essential to keeping machines up and running.

THINK ABOUT IT

▶ How do you imagine the machines of the future? Will millwrights still be needed? Explain your reasoning.
▶ Do you think trade jobs are important? Explain your answer.
▶ What are the benefits of learning both in a classroom and on the job?

GLOSSARY

apprenticeship (uh-PREN-tis-ship): An apprenticeship is a type of supervised work where someone learns trade skills. The student went into an apprenticeship program.

blueprints (BLOO-prints): Blueprints are detailed plans of how something will be built. The millwright looked at the machine's blueprints.

contaminate (kuhn-TAM-uh-nate): Contaminate means to make something dirty or poisonous. Untreated sewage can contaminate rivers and lakes.

journey worker (JUR-nee WUR-kur): A journey worker is a person who has learned a trade and is an experienced worker. The apprentice learned from the journey worker.

maintenance logs (MAY-tuh-nuhns LAWGZ): Maintenance logs are documents that keep track of work in order to keep something in good condition. It's important for technicians to keep maintenance logs up to date.

pendulum (PEN-juh-luhm): A pendulum is a weight that swings from side to side in a clock. Javier watched the grandfather clock's pendulum.

precision (pri-SIZH-uhn): Precision means to be exact. The millwright used a precision-measuring device in his work.

pulley (PUL-ee): A pulley is a piece of equipment to move objects up or down, usually with a rope or chain attached to the object, laying over a wheel. The pulley on the grandfather clock helped move the weights to set the time.

renewable energy (ri-NOO-uh-buhl EN-ur-jee): Renewable energy is a type of power source that can't be used up. Sources of renewable energy include solar, wind, and water.

TO LEARN MORE

BOOKS

Long, Paul. *Build Your Own Chain Reaction Machines.* Beverly, MA: Quarry Books, 2018.

Macaulay, David. *The Way Things Work Now.* Boston, MA: Houghton Mifflin Harcourt, 2016.

Resler, T. J. *Discover Secrets and Science Behind Bounce Houses, Hovercraft, Robotics, and Everything in Between.* Washington, DC: National Geographic, 2016.

WEBSITES

Visit our website for links about machines: **childsworld.com/links**

Note to Parents, Teachers, and Librarians: We routinely verify our Web links to make sure they are safe and active sites. So encourage your readers to check them out!

SELECTED BIBLIOGRAPHY

"Millwrights." *Bureau of Labor Statistics*, 29 Mar. 2019, bls.gov. Accessed 9 Apr. 2019.

"Millwrights." *United Brotherhood of Carpenters and Joiners of America*, n.d., carpenters.org. Accessed 9 Apr. 2019.

"Troubleshooting Wastewater Treatment Plants." *American Institute of Chemical Engineers*, Sept. 2017, aiche.org. Accessed 9 Apr. 2019.

INDEX

ABOUT THE AUTHOR

Heidi Ayarbe is an author, storyteller, and translator. She grew up in Nevada and has lived and traveled all over the world.